It's time to GO!
TO SCHOOL

By Torre and Torian Stocker

Copyright © 2022 by Torre A. Stocker
All rights reserved. This book or any portion thereof
may not be reproduced or used in any manner whatsoever without the express written
permission of the publisher except for the use of brief quotations in a book review.

Printed in the United States of America

First Edition, 2022

ISBN 978-0-5783-7939-5

Red Pen Edits and Consulting, LLC
P. O. Box 25283
Columbia, SC 29223
www.redpeneditsllc.com

DEDICATIONS

This book is dedicated to all of the students, administrators, faculty and staff members of Richland County's District Two Schools.

Summer vacation has come to an end

No more late nights with video games

It's time for a new school year

New teachers, new friends, new

names

We went to the beach with buckets
and shovels
Just to play in the sand
Even though we're returning to school
The fun doesn't have to end

We slept late every day and lounged around
Man! Wasn't that cool?
Set the alarm! We can't miss the bus
Maybe Dad will take me to school

6

My bookbag is packed.
My clothes are out
It's time to go to bed
I wonder what my classroom looks like
That's all that's in my head

8

I arrived at school
and see some old friends
We still have classes together
I can't wait to see my new teacher
And recess depending on the weather

The classroom is filled with books
and supplies
My name is written on my desk
My teacher goes over the
classroom rules
Raise your hand and
clean up your mess

Math, reading, and related arts
To learn is why we are here
"Would you like to hear more?", my
teacher says
We all let out a loud cheer

Classroom Rules

★ Raise Your Hand

★ Clean Your Mess

14

Before we know it, the final bell rings
Going home, I talk about my day
No homework, but I learned a lot
I have so much to share and say

16

Remember I said
that the fun doesn't end
School is a repeat of the same
There are so many people
that I want to meet
New teachers, new friends,
new names

After dinner and TV, I prepared for bed

Learning is my new cool

Rest tonight because in the morning

It's Time To GO To School!

ABOUT THE AUTHORS

TORRE A. STOCKER

Torre Antione Stocker is a results-seeking, life-long learner of leadership, vision pursuit, and entrepreneurial endeavors. **Torre**'s intellect and ability have been described as having an unprecedented brilliance to translate brainstorms into creative and innovative success tools and business models. Torre Stocker continues to be an active entrepreneur as *CEO* of **Torre A. Stocker, LLC (TAS, LLC)**, *Executive Director* of **Strategic Entrepreneur Empowerment (SEE)**, a registered 501(c)(3), tax-exempt non-profit organization in South Carolina and *CEO* of **Red Pen Edits and Consulting, LLC**.

Torre is a 7X author having released **"Success Moments: *50 Thoughts To Keep You Motivated*"**, **"A Graphic Designers Guide To Success: *What The Customer Wants and The Graphic Designer Needs*"**, **"The Power Of Go! - *How To Get From Where You Are To Where You Really Want To Be*" (Book and Workbook)** and four additional books from the current **"It's Time To Go!" Series**. **Torre A. Stocker** is a leader, consultant, and mentor with a wealth of knowledge to share.

Friend Torre On Facebook: www.facebook.com/torrestocker
Follow Torre On Twitter: @torrestocker - www.twitter.com/torrestocker
Follow Torre On Instagram: @torrestocker - www.instagram.com/torrestocker
Follow Torre On LinkedIn: Torre A. Stocker, MBA

TORIAN A. STOCKER

Torian Alexander Stocker, is the son of Torre and Triconya Stocker and younger brother of Angel Jacobs. **Torian** celebrates the release of more books from the "It's Time To GO!" Series, a collaborative effort with his father, Torre A. Stocker. **Torian Stocker** is an educational product of Richland County's District Two schools as he is matriculating through Windsor Elementary School (Columbia, SC). **Torian** extends his educational prowess as an ALERT student. In **Torian**'s spare time, he likes to read, play video games and watch television. **Torian** has expressed his early ambitions to be an Artist and Engineer as he likes to draw and create buildings, aircrafts and other brilliant creations using models and building blocks. **Torian** is properly positioned for the intentional acquisition of a legacy that is rooted in success and greatness.

Friend Torian On Facebook: www.facebook.com/torianstocker
Follow Torian On Instagram: @torianstocker - www.instagram.com/torianstocker
Follow It's Time To GO Book On Facebook: www.facebook.com/itstimetogobook

CPSIA information can be obtained
at www.ICGtesting.com
Printed in the USA
LVHW071628040422
715273LV00021B/762